THE TALE OF
Twinette
the Spider

For Jonathan, Peter and Amy

Text copyright © 1990 Pat Wynnejones
Illustrations copyright © 1990 Sheila Ratcliffe

Published by
Lion Publishing plc
Sandy Lane West, Oxford, England
ISBN 0 7459 1948 0
Lion Publishing Corporation
1705 Hubbard Avenue, Batavia, Illinois 60510, USA
ISBN 0 7459 1948 0
Albatross Books Pty Ltd
PO Box 320, Sutherland, NSW 2232, Australia
ISBN 0 7324 0230 1

First edition 1991

British Library Cataloguing in Publication Data
(Applied for)

Library of Congress Cataloging in Publication Data
(Applied for)

Printed and bound in Singapore

THE TALE OF
Twinette the Spider

Retold by Pat Wynnejones
from Mrs Gatty's 'Parables from Nature'

Illustrated by Sheila Ratcliffe

A LION BOOK

Oxford · Batavia · Sydney

It was the richest time of the year. Birds and squirrels were grateful for the hedgerows ripe with hips and haws, nuts and blackberries, for the fruitful cherry orchards and mossy branches laden with rosy apples. Fieldmice feasted on the fallen grains of corn among stubble rows, where scarlet poppies still flamed here and there. The mellow sun had now lifted the early mist from the meadows. It shone warmly on the red village rooftops and glinted from the gilded weather cock on the church tower.

Lin! Lan! Lone! The bells were pealing out across the harvested fields calling people to church. They made air currents that swayed the cobwebs in the belfry where Twinette the Spider lived.

Twinette was young, industrious and hungry. Her tummy was rumbling.

'Weave yourself a web, my dear,' advised her mother, 'and catch some flies for your dinner. You know how to without my telling you. Scramble along the rafters a little way and spin. But first let yourself down by the family rope and check that there is plenty of room below you for flies to fly in.'

Twinette was a very intelligent young spider, but something puzzled her.

'How will I know if there is enough space for the flies, Mother?'

'Dear me!' said her mother sharply. 'You with at least eight eyes in your head! Be off with you!'

Twinette scuttled off to the end of the rafter and began to prepare her rope. It was called a 'family rope' because Twinette's parents and grandparents had all made ropes in exactly the same way for generations. No one told them how to do it. They just knew.

'How clever I am!' thought Twinette, as the threads began to appear. 'How clever I am!' she thought as the threads twisted together to make a many-threaded rope. 'How clever I am!' she thought as she glued the ends of her rope onto the rafter – and twist! went the rope and down she went!

'Whee . . . eee . . . eee!' What fun it was to whizz down and then bounce up again on the end of her thread, to swing to and fro and round and round. And all the time she could not help thinking how very clever she was to do all these things without being taught.

'Is there space for the flies, I wonder?' she asked herself, twirling around, and she decided to investigate further.

As she ventured down she became aware that below her was a positive sea of colour and a most beautiful medley of sound. Twinette did not know it, but in the church below the Harvest Festival was in progress.

The sea of colour was the ladies' hats and dresses – pink and white, pale green and apricot, royal blue and crimson. There were little boys with carrotty curls, girls with raven ringlets or flaxen pigtails, and gentlemen with brown and fair and grey hair.

The whole church was splendid with fruit and flowers and sheaves of corn. There were mauve and purple Michaelmas daisies in tall vases, while along the window sills were ranged rows of apples, pears, grapes and even large marrows.

In front of the altar there was a huge loaf made in the shape of a sheaf of corn, and real sheaves were propped up on either side.

An exquisite perfume arose from all this array of flowers and fruit, and the singing rose up in a heavenly harmony.

> All things bright and beautiful,
> All creatures great and small,
> All things wise and wonderful,
> The Lord God made them all.

A small boy looked up and saw Twinette twirling around. He tugged at his mother's hand.

'Oh, Mamma,' he said, 'there *is* a "small creature" just above your head!' But 'Ssh, dear,' was all that his mother said.

The music came to an end, the church door opened, and as the people began to stream out into the sunshine a beautiful Red Admiral butterfly fluttered in and alighted on the Michaelmas daisies.

'Oh, do make yourself at home,' said Twinette, politely welcoming the visitor. For she looked on the church as her own home.

The butterfly did not reply at once. She knew that she was magnificent and she considered it an impertinence on the part of the plain little spider to speak to her at all.

At length she said haughtily, 'I am always at home on Michaelmas daisies. They are beautiful, just as I am beautiful. I only mingle with what is beautiful – certainly not with ugly little creatures dangling up and down on the end of a miserable thread!'

Twinette was astounded at this rudeness, but she was by no means shaken. She was quite as conceited as the butterfly, and in a moment was ready for the attack.

'There are thousands of creatures great and small who have coloured wings,' she replied. 'I think nothing of coloured wings, myself. It is much more special to be *wise* – and wonderful – like me.'

'Wise! Whatever makes you think that you are wise?'

'Well,' replied Twinette triumphantly, 'can you spin a web? I should just like to see you try. Now *I* can spin a web all by myself, without anyone showing me how. I'm the cleverest creature in the whole world ... the cleverest that has ever lived ... And as for this thread, I made it myself. No one told me what to do.'

A rough scratchy voice broke in on their elegant conversation.

'See that there marrer?' it said.

The voice came from a little brown harvest mouse that had run in from the fields in response to the wonderful smell of apples and bread from the church. Never before had he set eyes on such a feast, so he was thoroughly enjoying a nibble here and a mouthful there.

'See that there marrer?' repeated the mouse, picking his teeth with a straw and then using it to indicate an outsize marrow on the window ledge. 'Made it yerself, did yer? Made them apples, did yer?'

'Good gracious, no!' stammered Twinette.

'Made the snow in winter, the warmth to swell the grain, did yer, eh, did yer?' continued the mouse scornfully. 'Since you'm so clever maybe yer can tell me where all this fruit come from, and 'oo made the flowers, eh?'

He turned to the butterfly. 'And you, Missus 'igh an' Mighty – 'oo made yer glowing colours, eh? Tell me that!'

Twinette and the butterfly were both taken aback by the harvest mouse, his sudden interruption, his rough manner and the strange wisdom of his questions. It had begun to dawn on both of them that they had not acquired either their brains or their beauty unaided. Twinette was the first to recover.

'Well', she replied. 'What about you, eh? Do *you* know?'

'Tell yer this', said the mouse, giving a vulgar little belch. 'Twasn't me. Twasn't you, neither. There's someone bigger'n me and cleverer'n you that shows us what to do and how to do it – someone great and mighty 'oo makes it all, and 'oo makes all things well.'

The butterfly rose into the air and flew out among the ripe fruit in the gardens outside. She still knew that she was beautiful, but she felt grateful instead of feeling proud.

Twinette, remembering that she was hungry, returned to spin her web in the belfry, and remembered to be thankful for the flies that she caught for her dinner.

The little brown mouse continued his feast, his humble heart swelling with gratitude for all the beauty and wisdom and goodness that had made all things well.

The four stories in 'Village Tales' have been re-created from Mrs Gatty's 'Parables from Nature', first published in 1855. Mrs Gatty was a children's writer, and also a keen naturalist, who used stories from the world of nature to illustrate and communicate truths about God and his purposes. Each of the stories has a particular theme, based on a verse from the Bible.

In these modern versions, the stories have lost none of their original freshness and charm, and their message is as relevant today as when they were first written.

'The Tale of Twinette the Spider' takes as its theme the bountiful provision of God, who has created all things, giving them instinct, beauty, and all that they need. It is based on Psalm 104:24: 'O Lord, what a variety you have made! And in wisdom you have made them all! The earth is full of your riches.'